ORLAND PARK PUBLIC LIBRARY
3 1315 00439 3422

P9-DDL-283

A Really Good SNOWMAN

by Daniel J. Mahoney

Clarion Books
New York

Clarion Books
a Houghton Mifflin Company imprint
215 Park Avenue South, New York, NY 10003

The illustrations were executed in acrylic gouache.
The text was set in 15-point Stone Informal.

www.houghtonmifflinbooks.com

Printed in Singapore.

Library of Congress Cataloging-in-Publication Data

Mahoney, Daniel J., 1969–
A really good snowman / by Daniel J. Mahoney.
p. cm.
Summary: Jack does not always appreciate his little sister's assistance, but he comes to understand why she likes helping when she needs an extra set of paws to build her entry in the Shady Woods Snowman Contest.
ISBN 0-618-47554-0
1. Brothers and sisters—Fiction. 2. Helpfulness—Fiction. 3. Contests—Fiction. 4. Snowmen—Fiction. 5. Bears—Fiction.] I. Title.
PZ7.M27685Re 2005
[E]—dc22 2004020427

ISBN-13: 978-0-618-47554-4
ISBN-10: 0-618-47554-0

TWP 10 9 8 7 6 5 4 3 2 1

For my son, Ryan James, a really good baby

Jack was building a model plane. He was about to glue the wings on when he heard his sister, Nancy, coming up the stairs.

"Jack?" she called. "Oh, Jaa-aack!"

Jack darted into his closet and closed the door. He tried not to move. He tried not to breathe. If Nancy saw the plane, she'd want to help.

Nancy loved to help Jack. Once she'd helped him by cleaning his tuba.

Another time she'd helped him by illustrating his homework for science class.

And just yesterday she'd helped him shovel the driveway.

The closet door opened. “Hi, Jack,” said Nancy. “Are we playing hide-and-seek?”

“Uh, not exactly,” said Jack. He slipped the plane behind his back, but it was too late. Nancy had already spotted it.

"Oooh! I can help you build your plane," Nancy said. "I'll glue the wings on. I'm really good at gluing."

Jack shuddered. "Thanks, but I think I'll stop now," he said quickly. "I'm meeting Angie and Melden in the park. We're going to enter the Shady Woods Snowman Contest."

"Oooh! I'll come along and help," said Nancy. "I'm really good at making snowmen."

Jack just sighed.

By the time Jack and Nancy reached the park, Angie and Melden had already started. "Hi, guys," called Nancy. "I'm going to help you build your snowman."

Jack rolled his eyes. "Sorry," he said to his friends.

"That's okay," said Melden. "We can use the extra paws."

"Actually, we can't," said Angie. "The contest rules say only three to a team."

Suddenly, Jack felt more cheerful. "That's right," he told Nancy. "You'll have to build your own snowman."

SNOWMAN CONTEST
TODAY!

Nancy trudged off alone. For a moment, Jack was sorry. Then he turned his back and got to work.

Soon the park was filled with teams making snowmen.

There were happy snowmen and sad ones,

skinny ones and fat ones,

big ones and small ones.

And then there was Nancy's.

Clyde and his friends stopped to take a look. "What do you call *that?*" asked Clyde.

"A snowman," Nancy said proudly.

"A snow lump is more like it," jeered Clyde. "Here, we'll make it bigger for you."

"Stop!" yelled Nancy.

Jack saw what was happening and ran over. "Leave my sister alone!" he said.

"What's the big deal?" said Clyde. "We were just helping her out."

"She doesn't need your kind of help," said Jack.

"Yeah, what she needs is a miracle!" said Clyde, and he and his friends swaggered off, laughing.

Nancy looked at her snowman. “It’s ruined,” she said with a sniff.

“Don’t worry, we can fix it,” said Jack. “Come on. Let’s get started.”

Soon, Angie and Melden joined them.
“Hey, Jack. I thought you were on our team,” said Angie.
“Yeah,” said Melden. “What’s going on?”

Jack looked at his friends. He looked at his sister. Then he sighed. "You guys can build a snowman without me," he said. "Nancy can't."

"Good point," said Angie.

"Good luck!" said Melden. Then he and Angie went back to their snowman.

Nancy knew exactly what she wanted her snowman to look like.

So Jack piled snow up, and then she packed it down and smoothed it out and patted it into place.

"This is going to be a really good snowman," Jack said as it began to take shape.

Suddenly, he realized that he was having fun—and he understood why Nancy liked helping out.

Not that he planned to let her get within five feet of his model plane . . .

By the end of the afternoon, there were snowmen everywhere.

There were excited ones and grumpy ones,

brave ones and frightened ones,

smart ones and silly ones.

And then there was Nancy's.

It wasn't short or tall or weird or funny. It was just a regular, middle-sized snowman. But it was hers.

The judges walked around the park. They circled each snowman, jotting things down on their clipboards. Jack watched them anxiously. It would be so great for Nancy to win her very first snowman contest!

The judges made more notes on their clipboards.

They talked for a while.
Finally, they headed straight
toward Nancy and Jack . . .

. . . and straight past them. “The winners of the fifth annual Shady Woods Snowman Contest are . . . Angie and Melden!” announced the head judge, handing Angie the trophy.

1st PLACE
J
1 Angie
5 Sal
6 Martha
7 Fred
J

Everyone clapped and cheered. Some of the big kids hoisted Angie and Melden onto their shoulders and carried them all around the park.

1ST PLACE

For a moment, Jack felt bad. If he had stayed with his team, *he* would be sharing that trophy now. Then Nancy put her paw in his, and the two of them joined the parade.

"Maybe you didn't win," Jack said as they headed home a little later. "But you know something, Nancy? You really *are* good at making snowmen."

After dinner, Jack discovered that Nancy was good at making trophies, too.